MAGICAL CREATURES

Mermaid

by Heather DiLorenzo Williams

illustrated by Haylee Troncone

full tilt
PRESS

For Lauren, *who brought magic to everything she touched.*

Mermaid
Magical Creatures

Copyright © 2022
Published by Full Tilt Press
Written by Heather DiLorenzo Williams
Illustrated by Haylee Troncone
All rights reserved.

Printed in the United States of America.
No part of this book may be reproduced in any manner whatsoever without written permission,
except in the case of brief quotations embodied in critical articles and reviews.

Full Tilt Press
42964 Osgood Road
Fremont, CA 94539
readfulltilt.com

Full Tilt Press publications may be purchased for educational, business, or sales promotional use.

Editorial Credits

Design and layout by Sara Radka
Edited by Meghan Gottschall
Copyedited by Nikki Ramsay

Image Credits

Flickr: 1950sUnlimited, 8; Getty Images: colematt, 20, colematt, 22, Lena_graphics, 17, mariaflaya, 12,
Oksana Opanasenko, 22, sceka, 22, TayyART ,11, TopVectors, 22, yelet, 22; Newscom: akg-images, 13;
Pixabay: BA93, 3, OpenClipart-Vectors, 1, 9, Yuri_B, 4; Shutterstock: EleniMac, 21, Shafran, 16

ISBN: 978-1-62920-886-2 (library binding)
ISBN: 978-1-62920-930-2 (ePub)

CONTENTS

MEET THE

Mermaid

Mermaids are half-human water creatures. They have many special powers. People have been telling stories of mermaids for thousands of years.

What Do Mermaids Look Like?

The upper half of a mermaid's body is human. The bottom half looks like a fish's tail with a strong fin. Mermaids have glowing skin and long flowing hair.

Most mermaids are kind and friendly. Some are known to be rude and grumpy. Selkies and merrows are types of mermaids from Scotland and Ireland. Merrows are thought to have green hair. Selkies can change into seals.

In Florida, Weeki Wachee Springs State Park holds live mermaid shows. These shows have been taking place for more than 70 years. Women dressed as mermaids perform in an underwater cove surrounded by live fish.

MERMAID FEATURES

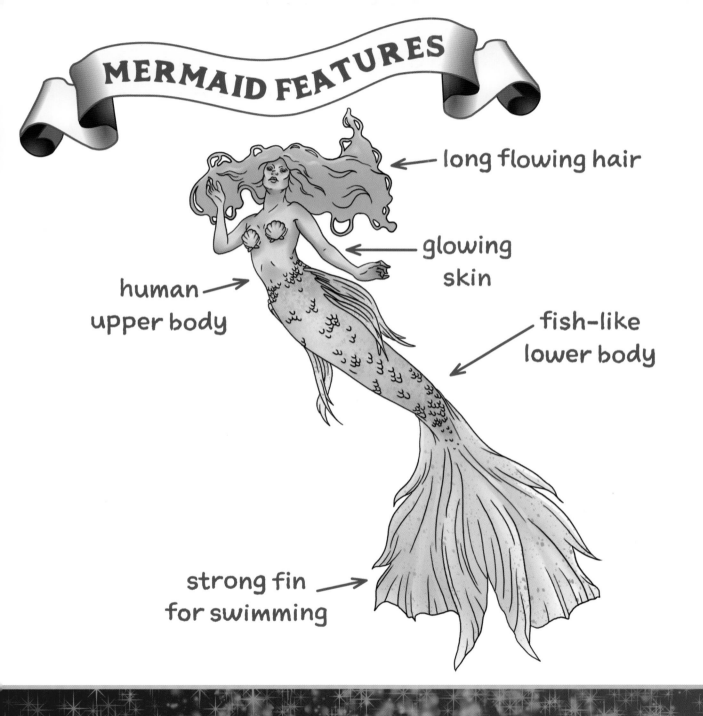

long flowing hair

glowing skin

human upper body

fish-like lower body

strong fin for swimming

Where Do Mermaids Live?

Mermaids live in the ocean. Sometimes they travel up rivers into lakes. They can be seen sitting on rocks near the shore. Mermaids use stone to build homes underwater. They live in communities with other mermaids.

Legends of mermaid-like creatures exist around the world. Mami Wata is a water spirit from Africa. Her name means "Mother of the Waters." Sirens were creatures from Ancient Greece. They lived near the water. Most sirens had wings. Some had tails like fish or feet like birds. They caused sailors to crash ships.

Some of the first maps had drawings of mermaids on them. They showed sailors where the water was **treacherous**. People thought these areas were the homes of sirens or angry mermaids.

treacherous: unpredictable and filled with danger

Sirens used their beautiful singing to make sailors steer their ships into rocks and crash.

Magical Powers

Mermaids have several magical powers. Their beautiful voices can put humans into a **trance**. Mermaids can also tell the future. They have powerful hearing. Some mermaids can also become **invisible**.

trance: a sleeplike state where a person cannot fully control their own mind

invisible: not able to be seen

Mermaids have power over water. They can freeze it or make it boiling hot. They can cause floods or storms when they are angry. Mermaids are much stronger than humans. They can also swim very fast.

Mermaids have been described as both beautiful and terrible. Many people believe they were **symbols** of the sea. The ocean could be smooth and calm one minute, and stormy and dangerous the next.

symbol: an object that stands for an idea or belief

Mermaids and Humans

Mermaids often befriend and marry humans. In one story, a mermaid named Ariel falls in love with a human. She trades her voice for legs so she can spend time with the man.

In some stories, mermaids **lure** sailors off course and cause them to crash. But mermaids are also known to save sailors from the water. They place them safely on land. The sailors can be found by other people. They will never forget meeting a mermaid!

The first mermaid sightings in North American waters were really **manatees**. The scientific name for manatees is *Sirenia*. This word relates to mermaid stories about sirens.

lure: to attract someone or something by promising a reward

manatee: a large water-dwelling mammal with a rounded back tail and front flippers

Mermaids who rescue sailors from shipwrecks are often honored as heroes in statues and paintings.

Fun Facts

A mermaid can live on land if a human **steals** something she owns. If she finds it, she must return to the sea.

Sounds made by boats are harmful to mermaids because their hearing is so **sensitive**.

 Mermaids are known to keep fish, sea horses, and other sea creatures as **pets**.

The words *merpeople* or *merfolk* refer to the whole **mermaid population**. Mermaids are female, and mermen are male.

Fire and sunlight can cause mermaids to die from **dehydration**.

QUIZ

1 What are mermaids from Scotland and Ireland called?

Selkies and merrows

2 What does "Mami Wata" mean?

Mother of the Waters

3 What kinds of things can mermaids do to water?

Freeze it, make it boiling hot

4 What were sailors really seeing when they claimed to see mermaids in North American waters?

Manatees

GLOSSARY

invisible: not able to be seen

lure: to attract someone or something by promising a reward

manatee: a large water-dwelling mammal with a rounded back tail and front flippers

superhuman: having powers greater than those of a regular person

symbol: an object that stands for an idea or belief

trance: a sleeplike state where a person cannot fully control their own mind

treacherous: unpredictable and filled with danger

READ MORE

Gish, Ashley. *Mermaids*. Mankato, MN: Creative Education, 2019.

Thorne, Russ. *The Magical History of Mermaids*. London: Flame Tree Publishing, 2018.

Mermaid Facts & Worksheets
https://kidskonnect.com/social-studies/mermaid/
This site includes many fun facts about the history, appearance, and magical powers of mermaids.

Mermaid Facts for Kids
https://kids.kiddle.co/Mermaid
This article contains a detailed history of the mermaids, as well as a variety of mermaid-themed artwork and architecture.

INDEX